Zeus and the
Dreadful Dragon

HEROES IN TRAINING

Zeus and the Dreadful Dragon

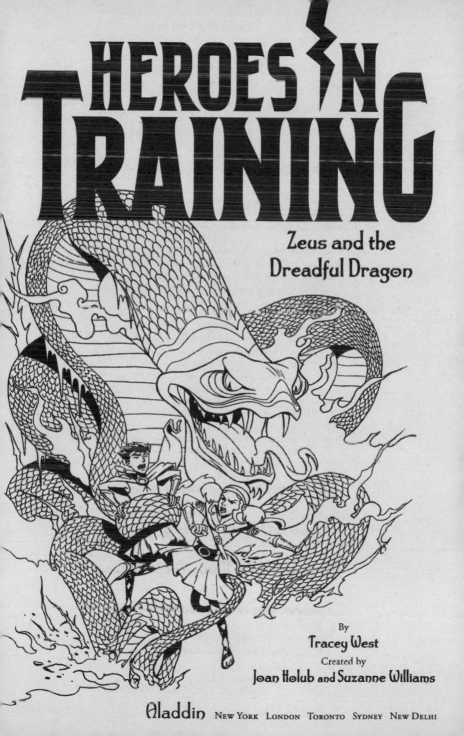

By
Tracey West

Created by
Joan Holub and Suzanne Williams

Aladdin   NEW YORK   LONDON   TORONTO   SYDNEY   NEW DELHI

ALADDIN

An imprint of Simon & Schuster Children's Publishing Division
1230 Avenue of the Americas, New York, NY 10020
First Aladdin paperback edition August 2018
Text copyright © 2018 by Joan Holub and Suzanne Williams
Illustrations copyright © 2018 by Craig Phillips
Also available in an Aladdin hardcover edition.
All rights reserved, including the right of reproduction
in whole or in part in any form.
ALADDIN and related logo are registered trademarks of Simon & Schuster, Inc.
For information about special discounts for bulk purchases,
please contact Simon & Schuster Special Sales
at 1-866-506-1949 or business@simonandschuster.com.
The Simon & Schuster Speakers Bureau can bring authors to your live event.
For more information or to book an event
contact the Simon & Schuster Speakers Bureau at 1-866-248-3049
or visit our website at www.simonspeakers.com.
Series designed by Karin Paprocki
Cover designed by Nina Simoneaux
Interior designed by Mike Rosamilia
The text of this book was set in Adobe Garamond Pro.
Manufactured in the United States of America 0718 OFF
2 4 6 8 10 9 7 5 3 1
Library of Congress Control Number 2018930870
ISBN 978-1-4814-8838-9 (hc)
ISBN 978-1-4814-8837-2 (pbk)
ISBN 978-1-4814-8839-6 (eBook)

⚡ Contents ⚡

Zeus and the Dreadful Dragon

Greetings,
Mortal Readers,

I am Pythia, the Oracle of Delphi, in Greece. I have the power to see the future. Hear my prophecy:

Ahead, I see dancers lurking. Wait—make that *danger* lurking. (The future can be blurry, especially when my eyeglasses are foggy.)

Anyhoo, beware! Titan giants seek to rule all of Earth's domains—oceans, mountains, forests, and the depths of the Underwear. Oops—make that *Underworld*. Led by King Cronus, they are out to destroy us all!

Yet I foresee hope. A band of rightful rulers called Olympians has begun to form. Though their size and youth are no match for the Titans, they are giant in heart, mind, and spirit. They follow their leader, Zeus, a very special boy. Zeus is destined to become king of the gods and ruler of the heavens.

If he is brave enough.

And if he and his friends work together as one. And if they can learn to use their new amazing flowers—um, amazing *powers*—in time to save the world!

CHAPTER ONE

A Flying Horse

"*The heroes are walking into danger.*

Not long ago we were all strangers.

Now we are a real fighting force.

One of us even has a flying horse!

This battle will be a real game changer—"

"Can you please stop singing, Apollo?" Hera asked the golden-haired boy. "We've got a long way to go, and if you're going to sing the whole time . . ."

Apollo stopped strumming his lyre. "Singing songs is what I do, but I will stop it just for you!" he replied.

"Thanks," Hera said. She turned to ten-year-old Zeus, who was walking next to her. "Okay, Boltbrain, what's the plan?"

The black-haired boy frowned. "I'm thinking."

"Well, you'd better start thinking faster, because we're on our way to face an army of Cronies, a family of Titans, and a father who wants to swallow us whole," Hera reminded him.

"I know that," Zeus said. "Just give me a minute!"

Not long ago Zeus had learned that he wasn't a normal boy. Pythia, an oracle at Delphi, had told him that he was an Olympian, a god, a hero in training. And he was destined to overthrow the mighty King Cronus and the Titans, who ruled Greece with cruelty and fear.

Pythia had also told Zeus that he couldn't do it alone. So for the last few months he had been on an epic journey to find the other Olympians—other immortal kids who were ten years old, just like him. Together they had battled monsters. They'd taken on the Cronies, King Cronus's army of half-giants. And they'd faced many Titans—giant gods with incredible powers.

Now all the Olympians were finally together, fourteen of them in all—plus four men with goat horns and hairy goat legs, who'd come with the newest Olympian, Dionysus. The Olympians even had help from a friend named Ron and his flying horse, Pegasus. But Hera was right. The battle ahead of them was a big one—an impossible one, even—and they needed a plan.

Zeus looked up and saw a white horse with wings flying toward them. He stopped, and the other Olympians stopped too.

The horse landed, and a boy with curly blond hair jumped off the horse's back.

"Did you see anything, Ron?" Zeus asked.

"There are pockets of Cronies between here and Mount Olympus," Ron reported. "It will be hard to avoid them."

Zeus nodded. "That's what I thought," he said. He turned to the others. "We're right on the coast. We should take a boat. It'll be safer—and faster."

"Um, why exactly would we want to get to Mount Olympus *faster*?" asked Poseidon, one of Zeus's brothers. "The Titans are there, waiting to smash us to smithereens. Not to mention that Ron heard there was an enormous dragon at Mount Titan."

"And how exactly is taking a boat safer?" asked Hera. "Won't Oceanus be waiting for us if we take a boat?"

Oceanus was one of the Titans—a big

golden-skinned giant who could harness the powers of the sea.

Ares stepped forward. "We've beaten Oceanus before! We can beat him again!" he said, shaking his fist. His red eyes were blazing.

Hephaestus snorted. "*We* didn't stop Oceanus last time. He got scared off when King Cronus started fighting with his dad, Uranus."

"We can still beat him!" Ares argued.

Athena, a serious-looking girl with gray eyes, spoke up. "Zeus, do we even need a boat?" she asked. "Apollo can make anything he sings about come true when he plays his golden lyre. Couldn't he just sing a song about us appearing at Mount Olympus?"

Zeus nodded. "I thought about that," he said. "But I think it's too risky. Apollo is just getting used to his new magical object. And if he sings the song a little bit wrong, somebody could get hurt."

 5

"What do you mean?" Athena asked.

"Well, if he sings about us appearing in Olympus, we might end up trapped inside the mountain," Zeus replied. "Or right on King Cronus's lap!"

"I hate to admit it, but Thunderpants has a point," Hera agreed. "It's too risky."

"And facing Oceanus isn't risky?" Hephaestus asked.

"Let's take a vote," suggested Hestia, one of Zeus's sisters.

Zeus was about to agree, but he stopped himself. He was a leader, and as a leader he had to do what was best for everybody. A vote might only lead to arguing.

"We're taking a boat," Zeus said firmly. He looked the other Olympians in the eyes. Nobody questioned him.

"There's a village just up ahead," Ron said. "We can get a boat there."

Hermes flew down from the sky, powered by his magical winged sandals. "I was just going to say that!" he said. Zeus had sent the flying Olympian to scout along with Ron. "It should be easy for us to find a boat to buy."

"Let's go, then," Zeus said. He started walking, and the others fell in step behind him.

Ron walked next to him, leading Pegasus.

"So, why does Hera call you 'Thunderboy' and 'Boltbrain' and 'Bolt Breath' and stuff like that?" he asked Zeus.

"It's because of Bolt," Zeus replied, patting the lightning bolt–shaped dagger tucked into his belt. He had pulled Bolt from a cone-shaped stone at Delphi. Even though many people had tried before him, Zeus had been the only one to pull Bolt free. Bolt was usually dagger-size, but it could grow up to five feet long—which was very useful!

Ron nodded. "I thought so, but she says those

names like having Bolt is a bad thing."

Zeus nodded. "And when she started doing it, she meant it that way. I think she was jealous."

"Jealous?" Ron asked.

"Well, every Olympian has at least one magical object," Zeus replied. "I got Bolt and Chip right away."

He looked down at Chip, the round, smooth stone pendant he wore around his neck. Chip was Zeus's other magical object, and it helped guide the Olympians in the right direction. The stone also spoke Chip Latin, which was like Pig Latin.

"But it took Hera a long time to get her magical peacock feather," Zeus continued. "And I think having to wait so long really bugged her. Now I think she just calls me names because she's used to doing it."

"Yeah, that makes sense," Ron said. He looked over at Pegasus. "I guess Pegasus is my magical object. Well, not an object, really. But you know. And I'm not even an Olympian!"

"Yeah, but we're glad you're with us," Zeus said. "I think we're going to need all the help we can get."

They had reached the village. Scattered small huts overlooked a sandy shoreline. Several boats bobbed in the turquoise sea, tied to a wooden dock.

Demeter, the third of Zeus's sisters, nodded to Zeus. "Aphrodite and I will try to get a boat," she said.

Aphrodite grinned and tossed her magical golden apple from one hand to the other. Gold coins showered down from the apple and landed at her feet.

"Do you think this will be enough?" she asked.

Demeter grinned. "Plenty," she said. "Let's go."

Minutes later the group was ready to sail away on a boat that fit all nineteen of them, and the horse as well. Aphrodite's bubbly charm and endless supply of gold had also helped buy a barrel of fresh water, six loaves of bread, two small wheels of cheese, and a parcel of salted fish.

Zeus watched as the Olympians boarded the boat. Hera, Hestia, and Demeter—his three sisters—stuck together like they always did. So did his brothers—Poseidon, god of the sea; and Hades, lord of the Underworld. The two boys were rolling the barrel of water up the ramp.

Then came the twins, Apollo and Artemis. Apollo's sister was as talented with a bow and arrow as Apollo was with his lyre.

Hermes flew over their heads. He was one of the newest Olympians, but Zeus suspected that with his magic staff he might be one of the most powerful.

Dionysus walked behind Apollo and Artemis. He looked more nervous than any of the rest, even though he was flanked by the four guys with goat horns—the members of his band.

I would be nervous too if I were him, Zeus thought. *Just last night he was the lead singer in a band. And now he's headed to meet the scary Titans!*

Athena and Aphrodite followed Dionysus, whispering to each other. When Aphrodite had first washed ashore in her shell, Athena had been a little wary of the newest addition to the group. But the two girls were now close.

And last came Ares and Hephaestus. Hephaestus leaned on his magnificent silver cane with the skull on top, glaring at the back of Ares's head as they walked on board.

Those two have never gotten along, Zeus thought. *But they'll have to start getting along very soon, or we'll never defeat King Cronus.*

"Are we ready to set sail?" Zeus asked.

"Aye, captain!" Poseidon called out, hoisting

the sails. "There's a good breeze today. Mount Titan, here we come!"

Ares, Hades, Artemis, and Hera each took an oar and steered the boat out of the port. Soon they were zipping up the coast, propelled by a light wind.

Zeus started to relax. The salt air gave him energy, and a yellow sun shone in the blue sky overhead. He walked over to Hera.

"Let's work on that plan now," he said. "I'm thinking—"

Suddenly the sailboat lurched. The calm waves around them began to churn.

With a mighty roar an enormous head rose from the waves: a head with long hair, a long beard, and angry eyes underneath green bushy eyebrows.

"Flipping fish sticks! It's Oceanus!" Poseidon cried.

Hera yelled, "Ha! I told you so!"

CHAPTER TWO

Grandma?

S plash!

A huge wave crashed over the side of the boat, knocking half the Olympians off their feet. As they scrambled to get up, a huge clawed hand shot from the waves and grabbed the boat.

With another thundering roar Oceanus lifted the boat right out of the water!

"Everyone, draw your magical items!" Zeus yelled, pulling Bolt from his belt.

The Titan held the boat right in front of his face.

"Well, well, well," he said in a deep voice. "I've got all the Olympians right in the palm of my hand!"

"Not for long!" Zeus cried. "Bolt, large!"

Bolt immediately grew into a lightning bolt larger than Zeus.

Oceanus pointed a finger at Zeus and hit the Olympian with a blast of water that drenched him.

"I'd be careful if I were you," Oceanus warned. "You don't want to zap yourself and your little friends here."

Ares ran forward, his red eyes blazing. "How do you like my spear, you big bully?" he yelled. He threw his spear at Oceanus. The spear bounced off the Titan's chest like a rubber ball and landed back in the boat.

 15

Oceanus chuckled. "Ha! That tickled," he said.

Artemis stepped forward. "I've got this." She started shooting silver arrows at the Titan. Some of them landed in his skin, but they didn't seem to bother him either.

Oceanus laughed again. "Is that really all you've got?" he taunted.

"Poseidon, your trident!" Zeus yelled to his brother. Poseidon's golden trident looked like a pitchfork, but it was a lot more fun and shot water on command.

"I can't fight water with water," Poseidon replied.

"And water beats fire," Hestia added, nodding to the magic torch she carried in her hand.

Zeus looked at Athena. "Can't you turn him into stone with your aegis?" he asked. Underneath the girl's cloak was a metal shield with the image of Medusa on it—a woman with snakes for hair. One look at it could turn someone into stone.

"It doesn't work on gods, remember?" Athena answered.

Zeus looked at Dionysus. The new Olympian could control minds with his song—but he had been knocked out cold by the wave. Next to Dionysus, Hermes was slowly sitting up and rubbing his head.

"We've got to try something," Zeus said, and Oceanus laughed above him. "Everybody, let's put our magical objects together! We can overpower him!"

Before anyone could do anything, though, Oceanus hit them with another water blast. This one knocked Zeus off his feet.

"Good luck with that," Oceanus roared, laughing. "Now it's off to King Cronus with you."

The salt water stung Zeus's eyes as he climbed to his feet. *This isn't how it's supposed to happen!* he thought. *It can't be over this soon!*

Then he heard a voice—a very loud, angry voice.

"Put them down, Oceanus."

Zeus looked toward the shore. A giant woman stood there, even taller than Oceanus. She had brown skin and wore green robes. Flowers and leaves were woven through her long, curly hair.

Oceanus's head spun around. "Mommy?"

Mommy? Zeus thought.

The woman stepped into the sea. "I mean it, Oceanus," she said firmly.

"But Cronus wants them," Oceanus whined.

The woman sighed. "Your brother is being very bad," the woman said. "Hand them over to me. Now!"

Suddenly the big golden Titan looked like a

scared little boy. With his head down, he handed the boat to the woman.

"Now go," she commanded.

Oceanus nodded and descended slowly into the water.

Zeus looked up at the woman. "Uh, thanks," he said. "Who are you?"

"I am Gaia," she replied. "Wife of Uranus. Mother of Cronus. And your grandmother, Zeus."

Grandmother?

As Zeus let this sink in, Hera stepped forward.

"Then you're *my* grandmother too," she said. "And Hestia's, Demeter's, Hades's, and Poseidon's."

Gaia smiled and nodded. "Yes. And that is why I want to help you defeat Cronus."

Hera's eyes narrowed. "Why would you want to help us take down your own kid?"

"Several reasons," Gaia replied. "Cronus cares

not for plants, nor clean air, nor clean water. I think you all will be better rulers of this planet."

Demeter spoke up. "I can promise you, we will be."

"And I am angry with Cronus," Gaia continued. "He has locked his three brothers in Tartarus for no good reason. Briar, Kottos, and Gyes are good boys. But Cronus is afraid of them, so he imprisoned them."

Hades got to his feet. "I can get them out of Tartarus," he said. "I'm ruler of the Underworld, you know."

"I know," Gaia said. "And if you free them, they will help you defeat Cronus."

Hera turned to Zeus. "I don't know if we can trust her," she said.

"Why not?" Zeus asked. "If she wanted to, she could bring us to Cronus right now. But she's not doing that."

He turned to Hades. "I'll go with you to the Underworld. In case you have any problems."

"The others will be safe with me," Gaia promised. "While you're gone, I can teach them about the Titans. It will be useful if you know their weaknesses."

"I'm all ears, Grandma!" Poseidon said happily.

Zeus nodded to Hades. "Let's go."

Hades clapped his hands. "Chariot, appear!"

A huge black hole opened up in the sky next to the boat. Four horses raced out of it, drawing a chariot behind them.

Hades and Zeus climbed into the chariot. "We'll be back soon," Zeus promised.

"You'd better be, Boltbrain!" Hera replied.

With that, the chariot disappeared into the black hole.

CHAPTER THREE

Three Hundred Hands

fter a few moments of flying, the chariot landed on the edge of a large pit. The stinky smell of sulfur rose from the abyss, and Hades inhaled deeply.

"Ahhhhh," he said happily. "Smells like home."

Zeus covered his nose with his hand. "That is a smell that only the lord of the Underworld could love," he said.

As he spoke, three women with wings flew up from the pit. One had a long pointy nose, another wore black pointy boots, and the third one had pointed ears. All three had wild hair and wore long flowing dresses. And after a closer look, Zeus remembered why their belts and bracelets were moving—because they were made of live snakes!

"Hello, my Furies," Hades said with a wave.

"Greetings, Lord Hades," the three Furies said together, bowing their heads. "How can we serve you?"

"We need to release three Titans from Tartarus," Hades replied. "But first maybe you can tell me how the other Titans got out?"

"It was not our fault, Lord Hades," said Pointy-Nose. "It was Thanatos. He—"

"LIES!"

A deep voice bellowed up from the pit, and a

man in a billowing gray cape floated up to the edge. The cape's hood hung low over his face, covering all but his angry mouth. Zeus and Hades had met him before. He was Thanatos, also known as Bringer of Death.

"We're not lying!" Pointy-Boots snapped. "You were supposed to be watching them while we went to that party at the Elysian Fields."

"We never get to go anywhere!" added Pointy-Ears.

"And you let us down!" finished Pointy-Nose. "But most of all you let down Lord Hades."

"I DID NOT!" Thanatos boomed. He waved his arms around wildly, and a huge gust of wind nearly knocked Hades and Zeus off their feet

"Uh-oh," Hades whispered. "Death-bringer dude sounds mad."

Thanatos continued to yell. "It's your fault! You didn't tell me you were going to the party.

You didn't even invite me." He pouted. "Nobody invites me anywhere."

"Ooookay. I'm sorry you missed the party," Hades said. "But there's nothing we can do about it now. And we need to get three Titans out of Tartarus."

"Briar, Kottos, and Gyes," Zeus added.

Pointy-Nose flew to hover in front of Hades. "You want us to let them out? But this is a *prison*! We're supposed to keep them in!"

"Yes, but their mom, Gaia, says they can help us defeat Cronus and the other Titans," Zeus explained.

"Are you sure you want this, Lord Hades?" Pointy-Boots asked.

"Yup," Hades replied.

"I will take you to them," Thanatos offered.

Thanatos dove into the pit, and Zeus and Hades followed him in the chariot. The air became warmer and smellier as they descended farther into the gloom.

At the bottom they glided over bubbling lava and then landed near the mouth of a large cave. Guarding the cave was a huge dog with three heads, dragon scales, and a tail that ended in a sharp point.

"Cerberus!" Hades cried happily, jumping out of the chariot. The dog creature ran to greet him, then began licking him with all three tongues. "I missed you, boy."

"He's never this happy when he sees me," Thanatos grumbled.

"That's because he likes me more," Hades teased. Cerberus gave another big lick, as if he agreed.

Before Thanatos could say anything else, Zeus climbed out of the chariot and walked up to Hades. "Come on. Let's see if we can find those three Titans."

They hadn't gone far into the cave when they heard voices arguing.

"I'm doing the left sleeve."

"No, *I'm* doing the left sleeve."

"You're both wrong. I'm doing the left sleeve."

The two boys gasped as they saw what was going on. The voices were coming from three Titans, but they were not like any Titans the boys had ever seen before. Each enormous being had lots and lots of arms—more arms than the boys could count! And every single arm was—knitting? An enormous wool sweater with a multitude of sleeves spilled out from under their knitting needles.

When the Titans saw the Olympians, every single knitting hand dropped. Each Titan had a long, shaggy beard. The only thing different about each one was the color of his eyes.

"Who goes there?" growled the blue-eyed brother.

"I am Hades, lord of the Underworld," Hades replied. "Are you the sons of Gaia? Briar, Kottos, and Gyes?"

"Yes, I'm Briar, but together we are known as the Hekatonkheires," the blue-eyed Titan replied. He pronounced it "heh-kah-TONK-eh-reez."

"The word 'Hekatonkheires' means 'one hundred hands,' in case you're wondering," the green-eyed brother informed Hades. "I'm Kottos."

"And I'm Gyes," said the brown-eyed brother. "Why are you guys here?"

"Your mom sent us to help break you out," Zeus explained.

Briar, Gyes, and Kottos stared at the two boys. "She did?" they asked.

Hades nodded. "Yeah. And since I'm lord of the Underworld, it's easy."

The three brothers looked at one another.

"Do you know what this means?" Briar asked his brothers.

"We sure do," Kottos replied.

There was a pause, and then all three yelled, "We can stop knitting this sweater!"

They jumped up and tossed their knitting needles onto the floor of the cave with joy.

"Why were you knitting this, anyway?" Zeus asked. "Is it a magical sweater?"

"Nope. It's a regular sweater," Gyes answered. "But you know, we've got three hundred hands between us, and so we need to keep them busy or we start hitting each other."

"Yeah, and that's no fun," Kottos added. "So we came up with a motto down here. 'Knitting, not hitting.'"

The three Titans were standing now, and Zeus was impressed. Each one was as tall as a tree, with enormous muscles. They would be a big help in fighting Cronus and the other Titans.

"You might have to do a little hitting when we get you out of here," Hades said. "Are you up for it?"

"Anything to get out of here!" replied the Hekatonkheires as one.

The group walked back to the cave entrance. Hades turned to Cerberus. "Sorry I have to go, boy. Don't worry. When this is all over, I'll be down here for good."

That was when it hit Zeus—all this time, they'd been focused on taking down King Cronus. He hadn't thought much about what would happen after that. He'd only met Hades— and the rest of the Olympians—a short time ago. And now it looked like winning against Cronus might mean that Zeus would lose his new friends and family.

Hades noticed Zeus's face. "Don't look so

down, Bro," he said. "We're going up! Portal, open!"

A black hole appeared in the cave. Hades and Zeus jumped back into the chariot. Hades nodded to the three Titans.

"Just jump through after us!" he told them.

The horses pulled the chariot through the portal. They emerged back on the beach, where Gaia and the other Olympians were waiting for them. One by one the three hundred-handed giants popped out of the portal.

The other Olympians looked shocked by the sight of the Hekatonkheires.

"Flipping fish sticks!" Poseidon cried. "That's a lot of hands!"

But the Titan brothers were too busy enjoying their freedom to notice the Olympians—or Gaia, who didn't look too happy that her sons were ignoring her!

The three Titans gazed around in wonder.

"Look at that blue sky!" Briar cried.

"Smell that salty air!" Kottos exclaimed.

"I see a field of flowers!" added Gyes.

Gaia frowned. "Aren't you happy to see your mother?"

The three Titans ignored her. They stomped down the coast, whooping and cheering about how happy they were to be free.

"Get back here right now, you three!" Gaia yelled, and she took off after them.

Hera looked at Zeus and shook her head. "I knew this whole thing was a trick!" she said.

CHAPTER FOUR

Two Old Ladies

I still don't think it was a trick," Zeus explained. He and the other Olympians were back on the boat, sailing the calm seas toward Mount Titan.

"Me neither," Hades agreed. "I think those guys just got excited to be out in the real world again. They'll come back."

"Well, they'd better come back," Hera

snapped. "Especially since Mr. Zappy here doesn't have a plan."

"That's not true," Zeus replied.

"Oh yeah? So, what is it?" Hera challenged him.

"Yes, what is it, fearless leader?" Hephaestus chimed in. Ever since they'd found Hephaestus, he had always wanted to be the leader of the group.

"We'll talk about it when we dock the boat later," Zeus replied.

"Right," Hera said. "Because you don't have a plan."

Zeus ignored her and stared out at the ocean. Hera was right. He didn't have a plan, exactly. When they got to Mount Titan, they'd be facing King Cronus, the other Titans, an army of Cronies, and maybe even monsters. How exactly did you plan for that? All he knew was that in the past everything had always worked out. He'd have to have faith in that.

Faith. That was the only plan he had. But he couldn't tell that to the others. He had to think of something.

They sailed all morning, and Poseidon docked the boat in the afternoon, before the sun set.

"It's about a half day's walk to Olympus from here," Hermes reported after returning from another scouting mission. "I don't think they're expecting us to come from the coast. Cronus has most of the Crony army stationed in the south and east."

Zeus nodded. "That's good," he said. "Maybe we can surprise them."

"Surprise? Is that your plan?" Hera asked, seeming to appear from nowhere.

Zeus changed the subject. "Ares and Hades,

tie the boat to the dock and then we'll eat. Who's hungry?"

"Me!" Poseidon yelled. "I'm so hungry, I could eat a fried boot!"

"We've got plenty of bread, cheese, and fish," Hestia said.

Demeter sighed. "I miss eating fresh fruit and vegetables."

Suddenly voices rose from below the dock. "Figs! Ripe, juicy figs!"

Demeter and Hestia raced to the edge of the boat. Down below were two gray-haired women in robes. One held a basket of plump purple figs.

"Yum!" Demeter cried. She turned to Aphrodite. "Could you please magic up a gold coin? Figs would be lovely for supper."

Aphrodite smiled. "Of course!" She tossed

her golden apple from hand to hand, and three gold coins clattered onto the deck.

Demeter picked up the coins and climbed down from the boat. A minute later she came back holding the basket of figs, followed by the two old women.

"This is Nemmy, and this is Risa," Demeter said. "They're giving us the whole basket of figs! I invited them to eat with us."

"The more the merrier!" Hades said.

"What a sweet young man you are," said Nemmy.

"Yes, such kind children," added Risa. "Please, eat some of our delicious figs."

Hades grabbed a fig from the basket and bit into it. "Mmm, juicy."

Most of the Olympians, Ron, and the four goat guys crowded around the basket of figs, happy to have fresh fruit to eat. Zeus didn't join them. He continued to gaze out at the waves, worried about the next day's battle.

Then he walked over to Poseidon. His brother's lips were purple from fig juice.

"Listen, Bro," Zeus said. "Hera is bugging me about a plan, and I think I have one."

"Hera? Who's Hera?" Poseidon asked, his eyes blank.

"Ha. Very funny, Poseidon," Zeus said.

"Poseidon? Who's that?" his brother asked.

Zeus sighed. He loved both of his brothers, but sometimes it was hard to get them to take things seriously.

"We need a plan for tomorrow," Zeus said. "For the battle with Cronus."

Poseidon just looked at him blankly, and that was when Zeus noticed that something wasn't quite right with him. He gazed around the boat. Hera, Apollo, Artemis—everyone he looked at was shuffling around the deck with wide, blank eyes.

He ran to Hera. "Hera! It's me, Zeus. Boltbrain!"

Hera looked confused. "Boltbrain?"

Zeus noticed that her lips were stained with purple too. That could only mean . . .

He turned to the two old ladies. They both were grinning at him.

"Would you like a fig, dear?" one of them asked sweetly.

"No!" Zeus cried, reaching for Bolt. "Those figs are messing with everybody's minds!"

He held Bolt out in front of him. His eyes widened as the air around the two old ladies began to shimmer.

Both women grew taller and taller until they towered over all the Olympians. Their wrinkles disappeared. The gray hair of one turned red, and the gray hair of the other turned black.

"Mnemosyne! Eris!" Zeus cried.

The two women were Titans, sisters of King Cronus. Zeus had met them before. In the Underworld, Mnemosyne had tricked Poseidon into drinking water that had erased his memory. And Eris had fed the Olympians food that had made them all angry with one another. Now it looked like the women had combined their powers into those dangerous figs.

Mnemosyne, the redhead, smiled. "You are a clever one, Zeus. But not clever enough. Your Olympians can't fight us if they can't remember they're Olympians!"

Eris, the dark-haired one, held out a fig. "Now be a good little boy and eat your fig," she said with a wicked laugh.

"No!" Zeus cried. "Bolt—"

Eris slapped Bolt out of his hands. Then she pinched his nose with two long fingers. His mouth opened instinctively.

"Open wide," she said.

Zeus struggled to break from her grasp. The fig touched his lips. Then, suddenly, something yanked Eris away from him.

The jolt knocked Zeus onto his back. When he stood up, he saw huge, thick green vines snaking around Eris and Mnemosyne. Demeter stepped out from behind them, smiling at Zeus.

"Demeter!" he cried. "You used one of your magic seeds?"

She nodded.

Zeus was puzzled. "But the figs?"

"I was being nice and handing them out to the others before I took mine," she replied. "Then I noticed that everyone was acting really weird."

The two Titans were struggling to get free of

the vines, but Zeus knew from experience that Demeter's magic monster vines were stronger than Titans.

Zeus yelled up at them. "What's the cure for your rotten figs?"

Eris laughed. "There is no cure!" she said. "Your friends will never remember who they are!"

CHAPTER FIVE
The Plan

The vines continued to grow around Eris and Mnemosyne, trapping them in a plant prison. Then the vines began to snake their way all over the boat.

"We've got to get everyone off!" Zeus yelled, and Demeter nodded. They quickly started to round up the others. Pegasus helped, pushing Ron forward with his nose.

"Where are we going?" mumbled Hades.

"Where are we now?" asked Ares.

Zeus and Demeter got the confused Olympians and the goat guys off the boat and onto the shore. The magical vines kept growing and growing. Finally, with one more loop, they took over the entire boat—trapping the two Titans inside!

"Let us out of here!" Mnemosyne yelled.

"Just wait until Cronus hears about this!" Eris wailed.

Zeus and Demeter ignored them as they did a quick check of the Olympians, who were all wandering around the beach in a daze.

"We've got to find some way to restore their memories," Zeus said. "Could one of your seeds help?"

Demeter frowned, thinking. "I suppose I could try to grow a flower with a cure, but I'm not sure that would work."

They were both silent for a moment, trying

to figure out what to do. Then they heard the sound of Apollo's golden lyre.

They turned to see the blond boy strumming his instrument, staring out at the waves.

"At least Apollo didn't forget how to play his lyre," Zeus remarked.

Demeter's eyes lit up. "Wait, that's it!" she said. "Just because he lost his memory doesn't mean he's lost his magic. When he sings about something and plays his lyre, it comes true!"

Zeus nodded excitedly. "I get it! We just need him to sing that everyone has their memory back, and it will happen," he said. "But how will we do that?"

"Let me try," Demeter said. She approached Apollo.

"Hi, Apollo. I'm Demeter," she said cheerfully.

He smiled at her. "Hello, Demeter. Who is Apollo?"

"You are Apollo," Demeter replied.

"Oh, I am?" he said, surprised. "That's a cool name."

"Can we play a little game?" Demeter asked. "How about I sing something, and you sing it back to me?"

Apollo nodded. "That sounds like fun!"

Demeter began to sing in a sweet voice. *"The Olympians and their friends lost their memories. . . ."*

"The Olympians and their friends lost their memories," Apollo repeated, strumming his lyre.

"But they will triumph over their enemies," Demeter sang.

"But they will triumph over their enemies."

"Their memories came back right away, and everyone was okay," Demeter finished.

Apollo sang and played, *"Their memories came back right away, and everyone was okay!"*

As soon as he sang the words, a light flickered in his eyes. "What do you know? I'm Apollo!"

The others began to talk all at once as their memories returned.

"What just happened?" Hera asked.

"How did we get onto the beach?" Athena wondered.

"Flipping fish sticks! Where did that giant plant come from?" Poseidon exclaimed.

"Settle down, everybody!" Zeus called out, and he quickly explained how they had been tricked, and how Demeter had saved them.

Hestia hugged her sister. "You are so smart!"

Demeter smiled. "It's just lucky that I didn't eat any of those figs."

Ares looked around. "It's getting dark. What should we do? We can't get back onto the boat."

"We can camp right here," Zeus said.

"I'll light a fire!" Hestia offered.

"And then what?" Hera wondered. She nodded to the two Titans trapped in the prison of vines. "What do we do about those two?"

Before Zeus could answer, Demeter spoke up.

"I don't think they'll be able to get out of those vines for a while," Demeter said. "When I planted the seed, I made sure to make the vines extra strong."

Hestia pointed her flaming torch at the pile of logs she had just gathered. A flame jumped out of the torch and immediately set the logs ablaze. "We can take turns watching the prison tonight and make sure the Titans don't get out," she offered.

Zeus nodded. "All right," he said. "We'll camp here for now and head out in the morning."

When the sun rose the next day, the two Titans were still safely trapped by the vines. Zeus sent

Hermes to scout out the road to Olympus. Hermes returned while the Olympians were eating whatever food they'd had in their packs when they had fled the boat: bread and a little bit of cheese.

"What did you see, Hermes?" Zeus asked.

"The road to Mount Olympus is blocked," Hermes reported. "There's a big wave of Cronies—about fifty or so, I'd say. Then a little farther down there are five big Titan guys. Behind them are two even bigger Titans. One keeps setting fire to everything."

"Sounds like Hyperion," Zeus remarked. "He used to be Cronus's second-in-command."

"Didn't Cronus banish Hyperion after we beat him?" Hera asked.

Zeus nodded. "Yeah, but Cronus probably realized that he needed Hyperion's help to defeat us."

"The other big guy was a big band of wind

with wings, and snakes instead of legs," Hermes added. "He was blowing stuff around with his stinky breath. I didn't get too close, but, boy, was it gross!"

"That's Typhon," Apollo said. "I was his prisoner for a while. He *is* a big bag of wind!"

"Is that all?" Zeus asked.

Hermes nodded. "Past Hyperion and Typhon is the palace on top of Mount Olympus," he said. "I couldn't see Cronus."

"What about the dragon that I heard about?" Ron asked. "It's supposed to be enormous!"

Hermes shook his head. "Maybe it's inside the palace? I didn't see it."

Hera folded her arms across her chest and looked at Zeus. "Now would be a good time to hear your plan, don't you think?"

Zeus almost snapped back at Hera but stopped just in time. She was right—they did need a plan. But he had been trying too hard to think of one all by himself. He remembered what his mom, Rhea, had told him, that he didn't always have to do things by himself.

He looked at Hera. "Maybe you can help me come up with a plan," he said. He looked at the others. "Maybe you all can."

The Olympians and Ron gathered around him in a circle. Zeus picked up a stick, crouched down, and drew a line in the sandy earth.

"The first wave is Cronies," he began. "Apollo and Dionysus, you guys got rid of a whole Crony army by combining your magic songs. So we'll put you on the front line."

"They'll need a few of us who can protect them if the Cronies attack," Hestia said. "I'll do it."

"And I'll use my slingshot," Demeter offered.

Zeus nodded. "Okay. That's you four," he

said. He drew another line. "Next, Hermes said there were five big Titan guys."

"That could be Iapetos, my dad—I mean, the guy who kidnapped me—and my four brothers. I mean, his four sons," Ares said. "They're mostly just big and strong. But I have my spear now. I can take them." He shook his spear to emphasize his point.

"You'll need help," Zeus said.

"I'll do it!" Poseidon offered.

"No," Hera said. "We'll need your water power to cool down Hyperion."

Zeus nodded. "Smart thinking," he said, and Hera's eyebrows raised in surprise at the compliment. Zeus started drawing more lines in the dirt. "Let's match our powers with the powers of the Titans. Aphrodite, you stick with Poseidon and take down Hyperion."

"Okay," she said, smiling at Poseidon.

"Artemis and Hermes, you two can focus on Typhon," Zeus went on. "And, Hephaestus, you stick with Ares."

"What?" Hephaestus cried, and Ares glared at Zeus. "Why?"

"Because I've seen what your cane can do," Zeus replied. "And combined with Ares's spear, you two should be unstoppable."

The two boys frowned, but they didn't argue with that.

"Hera, Athena, and Hades, you three will stick with me, and we'll try to press through and get to the palace," he said. "If the dragon is there, we'll combine our magic and try to take it down."

"And then what?" Hera asked.

"And then the fourteen of us will face Cronus together," Zeus said. "That's how it has to be."

"What about me?" Ron asked. "What can I do?"

"I'd like you to stay back here and guard Mnemosyne and Eris," Zeus said.

"But I can fight!" Ron protested.

Zeus nodded. "I know. But we're all basically immortal, and since you're not . . ."

"You'll be safer here," Hera finished. "And if they get out, or if anyone else comes toward Olympus, you can fly on Pegasus and warn us. You are our official lookout!"

Ron seemed to be satisfied with that.

"The Goat Guys will stay with you," Dionysus added. "I don't want anything to happen to my band."

Zeus turned to Hera. "You'll be my second-in-command," he said. "If anything happens to me, the others need to follow you."

He looked at the other Olympians. "Got that?"

Everyone nodded.

"Nothing's going to happen to you," Hera insisted, and for the first time he could hear in her voice how much his sister cared for him. He smiled at her.

"Yeah, Cronus is going down!" Ares whooped.

"All right. Let's get packed up," Zeus said. Then he held out his right arm, and the others did the same, piling their hands on top of one another.

"This is it," Zeus said. "Today is the day we defeat the Titans and King Cronus. Today is the day we take Mount Olympus. Today is the day we fulfill our destiny. Is everybody ready?"

"Ready!" they shouted.

CHAPTER SIX

The Battle Begins

The fourteen Olympians marched off on the road to Mount Olympus. Apollo, Dionysus, Hera, and Hestia walked at the front of the group, with Zeus and Demeter right behind them. Apollo and Dionysus were talking and singing.

"The Cronies all disappeared," Apollo sang. "*Then they* . . . What rhymes with 'disappeared'?"

"Um . . . 'weird'?" Dionysus replied. "'Feared'?"

Apollo nodded. "'Feared.' That might work."

Hera stared at them. "What are you two doing?" she asked.

"We're getting a song ready for when we meet the Cronies," Apollo replied. "We want to be prepared."

Zeus was surprised to hear that. Usually Apollo made up songs on the spur of the moment. If he was thinking up his lyrics before the battle, he was really taking this seriously.

Hera nodded. "Good," she said. "Carry on."

Zeus smiled. Hera was taking her job as second-in-command seriously too.

They'd been walking for about an hour when the tall peak of Mount Olympus appeared in the distance. Above the peak Cronus's glittering gold-and-marble temple on the palace grounds sat on top of thick, fluffy white clouds.

Zeus stopped. "There it is," he said. "The future home of the Olympians."

The others stopped and stared.

"Wow, that's really high," Ares remarked. "I don't think I could live all the way up there."

"It won't be my home," Hades said. "I'll be in the Underworld."

"And I'll be in the sea, I guess," Poseidon said.

Everyone was quiet for a minute. Finally Hera spoke up.

"Listen, Pythia says our destiny is to defeat Cronus," she reminded them. "So that's what we've gotta do. We can work out living arrangements later."

Everyone nodded and kept walking. They crested the top of a small hill.

"I think it's showtime," Apollo said, pointing down.

A large group of Cronies was gathered at the

bottom of the hill. The thickly muscled half-giants all wore loincloths and were carrying spears.

"Apollo, Dionysus, Hestia, charge up!" Zeus commanded.

Apollo held up his lyre. Dionysus held up his crown of ivy. Hestia held up her torch. The three Olympians touched their magical objects together.

Zap! Clink! Zing!

A bright light exploded as the objects touched. For a few minutes the objects would be super-charged.

And just in time. When the objects charged up, the Cronies spotted the bright light.

"Oh good. Snack time!" one of them yelled.

With a loud cry the wall of Cronies charged up the hill.

"First wave, attack!" Zeus yelled.

Demeter shot a rock from her slingshot at the Cronies.

Whack! It hit one of the Cronies smack in the middle of the forehead. He fell forward.

Hestia aimed her torch at the Cronies. Fireballs rained down on them and landed at their feet.

"Hit it, Dionysus!" Apollo called out.

Dionysus began to sing. *"Cronies, hear my song! Everybody stop and listen to Apollo. Oh yeah!"*

Amped up with extra power, Dionysus's voice carried over the attacking Cronies. They all stopped moving.

Then Apollo sang, *"What happened at the battle was just like magic! The Cronies disappeared, but it wasn't tragic. One by one they popped far away. Where they went, nobody can say!"*

Poof! The nearest Crony vanished into thin air.

"Moldy mackerels! They're vanishing!" Poseidon cried.

Then *poof!* Another one disappeared.

Apollo kept singing the song. Hestia looked at Zeus.

"Keep going!" she yelled. "We've got this!"

Zeus nodded and motioned for the other Olympians to follow him. They ran down the hill, around the Crony army. Looking behind him, Zeus saw the Cronies continuing to disappear one by one.

The road continued through a wooded area and emerged onto a field. When the group ran out onto the grass, they found five Titans waiting for them. The tallest one had a bushy brown beard streaked with white. He pointed at Ares.

"Slug! You are in so much trouble!" he yelled. "Come on over here, Son, so me and your brothers can punish you for what you did."

"I'm not your son, Iapetos, and they are not my brothers!" Ares yelled back. "You kidnapped me when I was a baby, remember? Now I'm with the Olympians, where I belong!"

"Why would you want to stick with a bunch of puny losers?" asked one of the Titans. Zeus remembered his name—Atlas.

Hephaestus stepped forward, walking with his skull-tipped cane. "Who are you calling a loser, you . . . loser!" he yelled.

Atlas laughed. "That's big talk, coming from a little pipsqueak," he scoffed, and Hephaestus's eyes narrowed.

"Ignore that kid. Get me Slug!" Iapetos demanded.

His four sons lunged forward. Ares stood, frozen, with a look of fear in his eyes. Seeing the five Titans, who had been so horrible to him when he was growing up, was definitely no fun for Ares. And Zeus could tell that Ares needed some help.

"Bolt, large!" Zeus cried, knowing he would have to protect Ares. But before he could do anything else, he saw Hephaestus's cane go flying through the air.

Whack! Whack! Whack! Whack! The cane hit each of the four brothers, knocking them backward. After the last brother was hit, the cane zoomed back to Hephaestus's hand.

Ares snapped out of his trance.

"Thanks," he said gratefully.

"I didn't do it for you," Hephaestus grumbled. "Well, maybe a little bit."

Ares and Hephaestus touched their magical weapons together and supercharged them as the four Titans struggled to their feet. Ares looked at Zeus with new confidence.

"Keep going!" he yelled. "We got this!"

"Are you sure?" Zeus asked. He glanced nervously over at the five Titans, who were back on their feet and looking at Ares with fury In their eyes.

"Sure!" Ares said, holding up his glowing spear. "And I can call in backup too."

Ares whistled, a loud piercing cry that carried over the hills. He used it to call for the Stymphalian birds. They weren't just any kind of bird; they were fierce and ready to fight. They were made of metal, and their poo was not just smelly—it was dangerous!

Hera tugged on Zeus's sleeve. "We'd better get out of here before the poison poop starts falling."

Zeus nodded and motioned for the remaining Olympians to follow, and they ran across the field. The last thing Zeus saw was Ares and Hephaestus giving each other a high five before they charged toward Iapetos and his sons. In the distance Zeus could hear the cry of the battle birds.

"This is where I saw the big blowhard guy and the fire guy," Hermes remarked as they climbed up another hill. "Right over this—whoaaaaaaa!"

A huge fireball exploded at his feet, but he jumped up in time to avoid it, and then hovered over the flames with his winged sandals.

"It's Hyperion!" Zeus yelled. "Poseidon! Aphrodite!"

"Trident, long!" Poseidon yelled. He held up his trident, and Aphrodite held up her golden apple, and the two magical objects charged up with extra power. A bright light exploded from them as Hyperion rushed up the hill.

The big Titan's body glowed like the sun. His red hair streamed behind him like the flames of a fire. A gold crown glittered on his head.

"Olympians! Bet you can't take the heat!" he growled. He opened his palm, and another fireball began to form.

 70

Aphrodite giggled. "Wow, that's pretty bright," she agreed. "But I have something brighter."

She held out her right hand, with the golden apple in her palm. A bright beam of light shone from it and hit Hyperion directly in the eyes.

"Hey, stop that!" the Titan cried. "I can't see!"

Frantic, he swatted at the light in front of his eyes.

Poseidon charged toward him. "You think you're so hot, but you're not!" he cried. "Time to cool down!"

Poseidon pointed his trident at Hyperion, and a wave of water shot from it, dousing the Titan.

"Where are you, you shrimpy brat?" Hyperion sputtered, fuming. "I'll fry you to a crisp!"

Poseidon blasted Hyperion with another wave of water, and Zeus started to feel confident.

"We are kicking Titan butt!" he yelled.

"Hera, Hades, Athena, Hermes, Artemis, let's keep going! We are going to—"

WHOOSH!

A huge wind swept up the hill, knocking the six Olympians off their feet!

CHAPTER SEVEN

And Then There Were Three

Typhon!" Zeus yelled, jumping back up.

Another terrible Titan slithered toward them. He had a craggy face with dark eyes and a shaggy black beard. Two wings covered with shiny black feathers grew from his muscled back. Instead of legs the lower half of his body was made up of a tangle of giant, living snakes.

"That is one ugly dude," Hermes remarked. He looked at Artemis. "He's ours, right?"

She nodded and held up her gold bow and the quiver of silver arrows. Hermes held up his staff, a golden rod with two wings at the top and snakes wrapped around it.

Boom! Light exploded as their weapons super-charged.

"Can't you turn him into a bird or something?" Artemis asked.

Hermes nodded. "I can if you distract him."

Artemis grinned. "No problem!" she said, and she ran toward Typhon, shooting arrows at supersonic speed.

"Hey! Quit it! Stop that!" Typhon bellowed, trying to bat the arrows away with his enormous arms. Some of the arrows landed in his arms and chest.

Hermes lifted off and started to fly over

Typhon. Zeus knew that Hermes's staff contained powerful magic. Zeus had no doubt that Hermes and Artemis could take on Typhon. He turned to Hades.

"Call up your chariot," he said. "Start bringing the fallen Titans to Tartarus. Then bring all the Olympians up to meet us at the temple."

"Will do, Bro!" Hades replied. He clapped his hands. "Chariot, appear!"

The swirling portal opened, and Hades's four horses flew out of it, pulling the chariot. Hades hopped on.

"See you soon!" he said, and then the chariot zipped away.

Now only Zeus, Hera, and Athena were left. They marched toward Mount Olympus. At the foot of the mountain Zeus stopped.

"Hera, send your feather to look ahead," Zeus said.

Hera held up a peacock feather—her magical object—and began to rhyme. It was how the magic in the feather worked, kind of like Apollo's lyre.

"Feather, up the mountain fly. Tell us what you spy with your eye!" she commanded.

The feather disappeared from her hand and flew away, up Mount Olympus. Zeus knew that the feather would return in a few minutes, and Hera would look into its eye and see a vision of exactly what the feather had seen.

Hera turned to Zeus.

"Is that why you made me your second-in command?" she asked. "Just so my feather could scout for you?"

Athena piped up. "I'm not sure why you brought me this far either," she said. "My aegis won't work against Cronus."

"But you always know what to do with your Thread of Cleverness," Zeus said, speaking of Athena's other magical object. "And you're smart. And brave."

He turned to Hera. "Just like you. You might not have a fancy weapon, but from the start you've been the bravest Olympian."

Hera blushed a little. "Well, thanks, Boltbrain," she said. "You can be smart too, when you want to be. And brave."

Athena started to pull the magical thread between her fingers. "If I really *were* smart, I'd be trying to figure out how to use the Thread of Cleverness to fight Cronus. Or that dragon Ron keeps talking about."

She scanned the ground and then picked up a long stick. Next she searched until she found a round, flat rock. She placed the two next to each other.

"This isn't exactly the best time for making crafts," Hera pointed out.

Athena placed the thread over the stick and rock. She started twisting the thread to spell two words: "spear" and "shield."

The rock and stick began to glow with magic. The stick bubbled and twisted into a long spear!

"Whoa!" yelled Hera.

The flat rock started to shimmy and smoke. After a few minutes it floated up into the air and then suddenly came back down with a *plink!* It had transformed into a shield of hammered metal.

"Wow, nice!" Zeus said.

"Something tells me I'm going to need some power—and some protection," Athena said. "What about you, Hera? Want me to clever you up a sword?"

Hera frowned thoughtfully. "Well, I've got my slingshot," she said. "But maybe—"

"Look! The feather!" Zeus cried, interrupting her.

The feather was speeding back down the mountain toward her—not just flying but speeding, as though it were being chased.

That was because it *was* being chased. An enormous dragon, whose head grazed the tree-tops when standing, slithered after the feather at magical speed. It had no legs, like a big snake, and shiny blue scales covered its body. Its huge jaws were open wide, revealing dozens of sharp teeth.

"It's the dragon!" Zeus yelled. "Bolt, large!"

CHAPTER EIGHT

The Unbeatable Dragon

olt instantly transformed from a short dagger into a large lightning bolt. The feather returned to Hera's hand, and she held it up. Athena added her Thread of Cleverness.

The dragon roared as the magical objects exploded in bright light. Athena held up her sword and spear. Hera pulled her slingshot out of her pack.

Zeus hurled Bolt with all his might. The sizzling lightning spear struck the dragon on the side of the head. The dragon's whole body trembled.

"Yes!" Zeus cheered. "First try!"

The jolt sent five of the dragon's teeth flying right out of its mouth! The creature let out a high-pitched screech.

"Bolt, again!" Zeus yelled.

Zap! Bolt struck the dragon, and its body sizzled. More of the dragon's teeth fell out of its mouth and landed in the dirt. The dragon thrashed angrily.

"Bolt—" Zeus began, but Athena interrupted him.

"Zeus, wait!" she cried out. "Look!"

To Zeus's horror, the dragon's teeth had transformed into soldiers! The soldiers wore shiny blue metal breastplates that looked like the dragon's scales. Each soldier wore a blue metal helmet and carried a big sword and a shield.

The soldiers growled and rushed forward to attack the Olympians.

"Bolt, return!" Zeus yelled, but Bolt had already zapped the dragon again. Twelve more teeth fell out, and twelve more soldiers sprang from the ground.

Athena removed her cape to expose the aegis. "Turn to stone!" she yelled at the soldiers.

But the aegis had no effect on them! They kept charging.

"Hera, behind me!" Athena cried. She held up her large shield and bravely kept the soldiers at bay with her spear.

Three of the soldiers converged on Zeus, their bright blue eyes glowing weirdly as they glared at him. Zeus held Bolt in front of him.

Zap! Zap! Zap! He struck each of them,

knocking them back. But they didn't stay down for long. Instead they sprang up again and kept coming!

"I can't hold them off much longer!" Athena cried. "They're unstoppable!"

"Bros to the rescue!"

Zeus spun around to see Hades driving up in his chariot. Ares, Hephaestus, Dionysus, Apollo, Aphrodite, Demeter, and Hestia rode in the carriage with him. Hermes flew overhead. And Artemis and Poseidon rode on the backs of the two chariot horses. Poseidon was waving his trident, which was still glowing with extra power.

"Hey, dirty dragon! Looks like you need a bath!" he yelled.

"Poseidon, no!" Zeus yelled, but Poseidon was already hitting the dragon with a heavy blast of water, right in the face! All of the dragon's teeth fell out this time—dozens of them. Each one that hit the ground turned into a warrior in blue armor.

The Olympians' jaws dropped.

"Oops. That's where those blue guys came from," Poseidon said. "My bad."

Artemis jumped off the horse and began shooting at the soldiers with her arrows. The projectiles just bounced off the skin of the soldiers.

"Ugh, this isn't working!" Artemis yelled in frustration. Hestia ran after her and started hurling fireballs at the soldiers' feet. But the dragon soldiers marched right through the flames, unhurt and not slowing down!

Hera jumped into the chariot and stood next to Demeter. Together they pelted the soldiers with stones from their slingshots. The stones bounced off their foreheads.

Apollo and Dionysus sang, *"The dragon soldiers dropped their swords!"* But the attackers didn't obey the song—they just kept coming!

Hermes flew above them, aiming his wand at each one. Zeus knew that Hermes could use his magic to turn just about anything into a bird. But like the other magical objects so far, the wand didn't seem to work on the dragon soldiers at all.

Zap! Zap! Zap! Zeus kept zapping them with Bolt, but the shocks did nothing. He grabbed his other magical object, Chip.

"Chip, is there any way to defeat these soldiers?" Zeus asked.

"Hey-tip are-ip as-ip ard-hip as-ip eeth-tip!" Chip replied.

"They are as hard as teeth," Zeus repeated. So that was why arrows couldn't pierce them, lightning couldn't shock them, magic didn't work on them, and fire couldn't burn them. It was why Athena's aegis didn't turn them into stone—the soldiers were already made of stuff as hard as stone. Zeus's stomach sank.

"They're teeth!" Zeus yelled to the others. "They can't be defeated!"

"Never say never!" Ares yelled, running toward the soldiers with his spear in hand. He reached back and threw his spear at one soldier, and it came right back to Ares like a boomerang.

Zeus hated to admit it, but he knew there was no way to get past the soldiers.

"Retreat!" he yelled. "Into the chariot!"

They ran for the chariot, with the soldiers in hot pursuit. The dragon screeched and lunged at Poseidon, and grabbed him in its toothless jaws.

"Let go of me, you big slimy worm!" Poseidon yelled.

Zeus's mind raced. Hades's chariot could take them to safety in a blink. But they couldn't leave Poseidon behind.

Just then Athena called out, "Hermes! The dragon isn't made of teeth. The dragon is flesh and blood!"

Hermes nodded. "Right!" he said. "I can transform it. But we need to get Poseidon out of there first."

"Got it," Hades said, jumping out of the chariot. He put on the Helm of Darkness and immediately turned invisible.

Zeus and the others continued to fight off the dragon soldiers as Hades and Hermes tried to save Poseidon. Zeus wasn't sure what Hades had in mind, but after a few seconds he saw the dragon start to shake. Then it began to make a sound in its throat, a sound almost like laughter.

Finally the dragon opened its mouth, and

Poseidon fell out and tumbled to the ground. Invisible hands pulled Poseidon away from the dragon. Above the dragon Hermes aimed his wand at the beast.

Sparkling white light flowed from the wand and hit the dragon. The dragon thrashed as the white light engulfed its body. Then the light exploded, blinding the Olympians.

When Zeus's eyes came into focus, he saw that the dragon's body had been transformed into an outline of sparkling stars. Hermes pointed his wand at the sky.

Whoosh! The stars flew up into the sky in the shape of the dragon. The Olympians cheered.

Then Zeus heard Hades's voice. "Good thing that dragon was ticklish!"

Hera tapped Zeus on the shoulder. "Do we have to leave?" she asked.

Zeus nodded. "We can't defeat the soldiers. We have to go. We'll find some other way to get to Cronus."

She nodded and started to gather the Olympians into the chariot. Artemis was still shooting arrows, trying to slow down the dragon soldiers.

Zeus didn't want to retreat, but there was no other way. They had failed. But maybe Pythia had had something else in mind. Maybe this was how things were supposed to happen.

Suddenly the ground beneath his feet began to shake. He heard loud thumps behind him and whirled around to see Briar, Kottos, and Gyes—the three sons of Gaia!

CHAPTER NINE

The Heart of a Hero

om said we have to come help you,"
Briar said in a defeated voice.

"Great!" Zeus said. "But I don't know
what you can do. These soldiers are as hard as
teeth. We can't—"

Kottos bent down and picked up one soldier
each in four of his one hundred hands. Then he
squeezed.

Poof! The crushed soldiers turned into white, chalk-like dust.

"They might be hard, but our hands are strong," Kottos said.

"Awesome!" Ares cheered.

"Yeah, so if you can get rid of these guys for us, that would be great," Zeus said.

"No problem," Gyes answered. "This is more fun than knitting!"

"Hitting, not knitting!" cheered the three brothers.

The three Titans mowed through the soldiers, grabbing them with their strong hands and crushing them into powder.

Zeus jumped into the chariot, where the rest of the Olympians were waiting.

"Hades?" Zeus said, looking around. "Can you get us to the top of the mountain?"

"Sure!" said a voice next to him. His brother was still invisible. The reins moved, and the four horses sprang forward.

"No biggie, but are you planning on staying invisible, Bro?" Poseidon asked.

"Well, we're going to face Cronus, right?" Hades asked. "It just seems like a smart idea to keep my helmet on."

Zeus couldn't argue. Cronus was the most powerful Titan, and the cruelest of them all. When Zeus's brothers and sisters had been born, Cronus had swallowed them whole, like they were lunch! Only Zeus had been spared, hidden away by their mother, Rhea.

The horses galloped up the mountain. The air grew colder and thinner as the group got closer to the clouds. The chariot landed in the courtyard of a majestic palace, on a cloud that spiraled high into the sky. Across the courtyard

of gleaming white marble, two Titans sat on shiny golden thrones adorned with jewels.

One Titan was a mountain of a man with bushy black hair and a gold crown on top of his head. Next to him was a woman with brown hair coiled around her head in braids. Her brown eyes looked sad.

"Cronus," Zeus said. "Rhea." He held Bolt in front of him, ready to strike Cronus down if he had to.

Cronus laughed, revealing a missing tooth in his large mouth. "Are you little toddlers here to try to battle me?" he said. "Now, that's funny."

"There's nothing funny about it!" Hera called out. "We defeated the other Titans. We defeated your dragon. Now we're going to defeat you."

The smile disappeared from Cronus's face. "Oh, are you?" he asked. He stood up and pointed at the Olympians. All but Zeus started to float in the air, helpless to resist Cronus's strong, ancient powers. They landed on a cloud floating above the temple, and the wisps of the cloud wrapped around their bodies.

"Flipping fish sticks! I can't move!" Poseidon yelled.

Zeus could see that their arms were trapped in the cloud. None of them could use their magical objects.

Zeus jumped out of the chariot and charged toward Cronus, brandishing Bolt.

"Let them go!" Zeus yelled.

"I can," Cronus replied calmly. "With a flick of my finger I can release them, sending them falling all the way down off this cloud."

Zeus paused.

"There's only one way you can stop me,"

Cronus said. "Take your place with me here on Mount Olympus. Rule with me."

"You asked me to do that once before," Zeus said. "And I refused."

Cronus's eyes flashed with anger. "I am not asking you," he said. "I am telling you."

"And I am telling *you*, I won't do it," Zeus replied. "I won't rule with you and the Titans and make everyone our slaves. It's not right."

Zeus looked at Rhea. "You don't want this either, do you?"

"I do not, my son," Rhea replied. "I have tried to sway your father, but he is unmoving."

"Help me convince him," Zeus pleaded. "Help me convince him that he's wrong!"

Cronus stood up. "Enough!" he bellowed. "I'm the ruler! I'm the one in charge here! You have no choice!"

He pointed his finger at the cloud, and it

plummeted. The Olympians screamed as they hurtled toward the ground.

Rhea jumped up. "My children!" she cried, and she leaped off the cloud, following them.

Zeus was stunned for a split second. Then rage exploded inside him.

"NOOOOOOOOOOO!" he thundered. He charged at Cronus and struck him with Bolt. An enormous shock rippled through the Titan's body.

Zeus had battled Cronus once before. He knew he could win. Before, Rhea had stopped him from harming his father.

But Rhea was gone.

A fury and strength that Zeus had never felt before rose inside him. Cronus pointed both hands at him, but Zeus hurled himself at his father and jumped onto the Titan's chest. He knocked Cronus flat onto his back.

"Stop this!" Cronus yelled.

"NO!" Zeus cried. "I must put a stop to YOU! Once and for all!"

He zapped Cronus again, and the Titan's body sparked and shuddered. Zeus climbed up to his father's face and pinned Bolt to his forehead.

"You are only this strong because of me, Zeus," Cronus said. "Don't ignore your destiny. I can show you how to harness your power! Together we can be great!"

Zeus's heart was pounding. One command to Bolt, and Zeus could silence Cronus forever. That was supposed to be Zeus's destiny, wasn't it? To take Cronus's place? Wasn't that the whole reason for his journey?

"Bolt!" he cried, and then, to his surprise, a black, swirling portal appeared behind Cronus.

Zeus heard Hades in his ear. "He didn't get me, Bro!"

Sweat poured down Zeus's face. With the help of Bolt, he could send Cronus through the portal that Hades had created, and into Tartarus. But what if Cronus escaped? Wouldn't it be better to finish him off so that there would be no chance of his coming back?

Then Zeus heard his mother's voice in his head. *Everybody has the potential inside them to be good or evil,* she had told him. *What matters are the choices we make.*

Zeus understood that. But sometimes, knowing the difference between a good choice and a bad one wasn't so easy.

Still, he had to choose.

"Release me, Son!" Cronus cried. "Rule with me!"

With a deep breath, Zeus made his choice.

CHAPTER TEN

Mount Olympus

With the strength of a thousand thunderclaps, Zeus pushed Cronus. The Titan stumbled backward and fell into the portal.

"Noooooooooooo!" Cronus wailed as the portal sucked him in.

Zeus stared at the swirling black hole, wondering if he had done the right thing. Hades removed his helmet.

"He should be stuck down there for a while," Hades said. "The Furies are all riled up, and Thanatos is happy to have a bunch of prisoners again."

"I hope they can hold the Titans," Zeus said, frowning. And then he realized something. "The others!"

He ran to the edge of the cloud and looked down, but all he could see were clouds floating below. Hot tears filled his eyes. Even though he had just gotten rid of Cronus, it didn't matter if the entire group was still out there.

"They're . . . they're gone," he said quietly.

"Looking for us, Bro?"

Zeus whirled around at the sound of Poseidon's voice. The god of the sea was clutched in one of Briar's hands. The other hundred-handed giants marched next to Briar. Between the three of them, they held each and every Olympian!

Zeus's heart leaped. Poseidon jumped down from Briar's hand, and Zeus hugged him.

"You guys are okay!" Zeus cried.

Poseidon nodded. "These guys are good catchers," he said.

"I guess you could say they came in *handy*, then," Hades joked.

"Rhea helped," Hera said. "She swooped down and grabbed the cloud, and that slowed us down as we fell."

"Is she okay too?" Zeus asked, and as he spoke, Rhea stepped out from between the giants, smiling.

Zeus ran into her open arms. "You're all right!" he said.

She nodded. "Yes. Are you?"

Zeus motioned toward the portal. "Yes," he said. "Cronus is still alive. He's in Tartarus."

"And I shall follow him," she said. "Hades,

your Furies will need some help keeping the Titans imprisoned this time."

Hera, Demeter, and Hestia ran up to her. "But you're our mom, and we hardly even know you! Can't you stay?" Hera asked.

Rhea shook her head. "I wish I could," she said. "But for too long I stood by while Cronus did bad things. Now I must make sure he can never harm anyone again."

She hugged each of the girls and then called Poseidon over.

"I must say good-bye to you too, Poseidon," she said. Then she turned in the direction of Hades. "Maybe you'll let your brothers and sisters come visit me once in a while."

"Of course, Mom!" Hades said. He took off his helmet and turned to Zeus. "I guess I've got to go back to the Underworld. Now that, you know, everything is over."

"Yeah, I guess," Zeus said, and he started to feel sad. He had known for only a short time that Hades was his brother. Zeus didn't want to lose him now. He took a deep breath. "So, goodbye. For now."

"For now," Hades said. Then he smiled. "Hey, have you heard that the Underworld is really popular? People are *dying* to get in."

Zeus groaned. "I'm going to miss your awful jokes," he said.

"I'm not," Hera said. "But I will miss *you*." She gave Hades a tight squeeze.

While the Olympians took turns saying goodbye to Hades, Rhea turned to the three giants.

"I need you three to come with me," she said. "We'll need all the extra hands we can get to keep the Titans in line."

Briar brightened up. "You mean we'll have an important job?" he asked.

"Yes," Rhea replied. "Gaia will be very proud of you."

The three brothers looked at one another and nodded.

"More hitting!" Briar cheered.

"But not each other," Kottos added. "Just the other Titans."

"Do we have to stop knitting, though?" Gyes asked. "I kind of liked it."

"I'm sure you'll have time for knitting *and* hitting," Rhea said, with a twinkle in her eye.

"Hooray!" they shouted, and they jumped into the portal.

Rhea and Hades climbed into the chariot. "Come visit soon, everybody!" Hades called out. He steered the chariot into the portal, and then it closed behind him.

Hera turned to Zeus. "What now, Boltbrain?" she asked.

"Maybe you can stop calling me that, since I'm, like, the main ruler now," Zeus said.

"Main ruler of what, exactly?" Hera asked, her hands on her hips.

Zeus had to think about it. "Well, Greece, I guess," he replied. "Pythia said we were all supposed to rule in place of the Titans."

As he spoke, Pegasus flew up onto the cloud, with Ron on his back.

"Hey, you guys did it!" Ron said. "All the villagers down there are really excited. Everybody wants to know what you're going to do next."

"Next?" Zeus asked. "We just defeated the Titans. We've been fighting huge creatures and running and being hungry and cold and tired for . . . well, what feels like forever.

The other Olympians nodded.

Zeus continued, "So I think what we're going

to do next is take a nap! And get a snack—I'm hungry!"

Everyone cheered at that.

Ares started to run up the castle steps. "I call first dibs on a bedroom!" he yelled.

Hephaestus started to follow him. "No fair!"

Poseidon sighed. "I'd like to be able to hang out here with you guys in the palace," he said. "But I guess I've got to go be lord of the sea. And swim around with the fish and stuff."

Ares stopped running and spun around. "Hey, why does Poseidon get to rule all the oceans? Can't I rule something big too?"

"You're the god of war," Zeus reminded him. "That's a pretty big deal."

"Yeah, but war isn't a *place*," Ares said. "I'd like to rule a place, like the ocean or the Underworld. Or volcanoes or something."

"If anyone is going to rule volcanoes, it's going to be me!" Hephaestus argued. "I lived on a volcanic island for years."

Everyone started talking and arguing at once. Zeus was beginning to wonder how hard being the ruler of everything was going to be.

"So, what should I tell the villagers?" Ron asked.

Zeus thought. He took a deep breath. "Silence!" he boomed as loudly as he could, and everyone quieted down. "Ron, tell the villagers that from here on in, this mountain shall be home of the Olympians!"

The Olympians let out another cheer.

"And if the villagers have a problem, they can call on the Olympians for help," Zeus declared. "But . . . ask them to wait for a couple of days. We need a vacation!"

"Got it," Ron said, and then he flew off.

Poseidon's stomach growled. "Do you think there's any food in that temple? Fighting monsters makes me hungry!"

"Let's find out," Hestia suggested.

As they moved toward the palace stairs, a foggy mist appeared at the top. A woman appeared in the mist. She had long black hair and wore wire spectacles.

"Olympians! You did it!" she said, smiling. "Congratulations!"

"Nice to see you, Pythia," Zeus said. "And we couldn't have done it without you."

"It's good to see you smiling," Poseidon said. "Usually when you show up, it's to send us off on some dangerous and super-tiring adventure."

Pythia laughed. "Ha! I suppose that's true,"

she said. "But don't worry. I'm not sending you off anywhere."

"Thank goodness," Zeus said.

"No. This time the danger is coming to *you*," she said cheerfully. "A farmer is on its way to Mount Olympus!"

"A farmer?" Hera asked. "That doesn't sound too dangerous."

Pythia cleaned her glasses with her cloak. "Erm, sorry. My glasses were a little foggy. I mean an armadillo."

"But armadillos are cute," Athena said.

Pythia cleaned her glasses one more time. "Oh, here we go. An *army*. Yes, an army is headed to Mount Olympus!"

Zeus groaned. "I guess there's no time to rest when you're an Olympian!"

Maybe they wouldn't get a vacation. But for

the first time, Zeus realized, he wasn't scared or worried about one of Pythia's predictions.

All the Olympians were together now. It didn't matter if Hades lived in the Underworld, or Poseidon lived in the sea. They were still a team. They were stronger together—and better than ever!

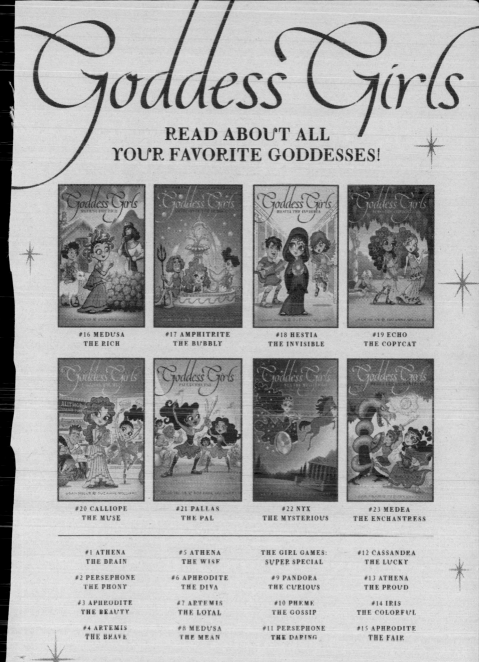

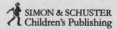